With Love

Annmarie.

KAI

An Altogether Improbable Love Story

Anne Marie Bennstrom

Hillsboro, Oregon

BEYOND WORDS
20827 N.W. Cornell Road, Suite 500
Hillsboro, Oregon 97124-9808
503-531-8700 / 503-531-8773 fax
www.beyondword.com

Chapter illustrations: Jim Loftus
Cover illustrations: Jim Loftus and Jeanette Little
Design: Devon Smith
Composition: William H. Brunson Typography Services

First Beyond Words trade paperback edition December 2013
Beyond Words Publishing is an imprint of Simon & Schuster, Inc. and the Beyond Words logo is a registered trademark of Beyond Words Publishing, Inc.

For more information about special discounts for bulk purchases, please contact Beyond Words Special Sales at 503-531-8700 or specialsales@beyondwords.com.

Manufactured in the United States of America

10 9 8 7 6 5 4 3 2 1

Library of Congress Cataloging-in-Publication Data:
Bennstrom, Anne Marie.
Kai : an Altogether Improbable Love Story / Anne Marie Bennstrom. -- First Beyond Words trade paperback edition.
pages cm
1. Fables. 2. Didactic fiction. I. Title.
PS3602.E48K35 2013
813'.6--dc23

2013031408

ISBN 978-1-58270-480-7
ISBN 978-1-58270-501-9 (ebook)

The corporate mission of Beyond Words Publishing, Inc.: *Inspire to Integrity*

To the great adventure called Life.
May we all live it in the spirit of
thanksgiving, joy, and wonderment.

And in memory of Cynthia Black, publisher,
visionary, and friend, who passed this world
just as *KAI* was about to be sent to the printer.
You will be missed.

So be wise (cunning, shrewd, prudent, astute) as serpents
and innocent (harmless, simple) as doves.

—Matthew 10:16

FOREWORD

I deeply adore *Kai*. It is an important fable, not at all ordinary. I wept deeply from tenderness when I first read it. I was overcome with love for this snake, and I realized it is a story for all of us, at any age. It is timely that it is coming into the world now, as our world is learning to forgive the unforgivable, in each other and ourselves. *Kai* shows us the heart of the wounded, the ignorant, and the unloved, and it reveals that redemption belongs to us all. This utterly lovely tale illuminates, in a real and enchanting way, how a hardened heart can heal through loving . . . and that Loving is the Way.

—Leigh Taylor-Young,
Emmy Award–winning actress,
lover of spirit, nature, and the good in all

FOREWORD

Kai is the tale of a handicapped bird, a terrifying snake, and a wise and savvy sage—an unlikely cast of characters to say the least, but all chosen for a reason.

When Anne Marie was eleven, she and a buddy were out playing with a recently acquired slingshot. Standing on a balcony overlooking her yard, she saw a small finch on a birch tree in the distance. Impulsively, and wishing to show off to her friend, she quickly placed a stone in the sling, drew it back, and let it fly. To her amazement and horror, she hit the small creature and watched as it fell to the ground, writhed in pain for a few moments, and then died. Heartbroken, she buried the bird in her backyard. The experience left a scar on her tender psyche. She would forever afterward be a staunch protector and defender of all of Nature's critters, large and small.

Many years later, as a young woman in her twenties and yearning for adventure, she decided to leave her comfortable Los Angeles lifestyle and live alone in a Guatemalan rainforest for six months, braving the dense jungle barefoot and in only a bikini, carrying nothing but a poncho, a machete, and a few toiletries. She considered herself a nature girl, and she wanted to learn the ways of Mother Nature.

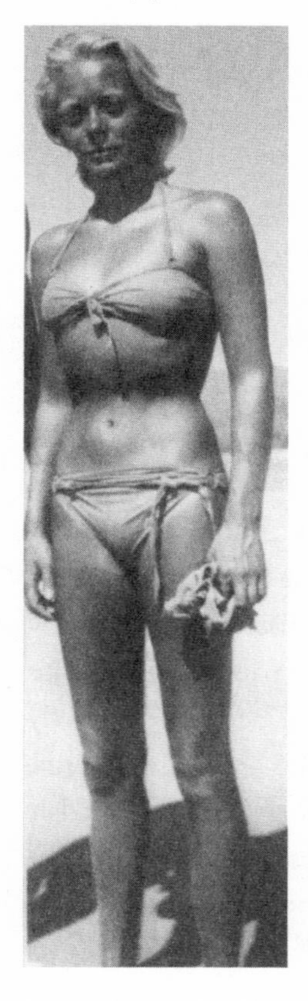

One day after many weeks in the jungle, Anne Marie was sitting against a towering tree when a gigantic "thing" happened down the trunk she was leaning against and began crossing her left shoulder. She remembers it being cool to the touch. She froze as the head of a snake came into view a few inches from her face. Without moving or making so much as a whisper of protest, she allowed the snake to make its way slowly over the length of her body. After what seemed like an eternity, it finally passed over her and continued to wind its way along the jungle floor. Afterward, she has a memory of missing it.

As the large snake crawled over her body that day, Anne Marie had to make a quick decision. It's usually referred to as the fight-or-flight instinct. We humans have been conditioned into believing that there are only two options when faced with a potentially dangerous situation: retaliate or run. Anne Marie inadvertently discovered another option. She chose to do nothing. She chose to simply observe the unfolding event from the impartial perspective of the observer. That basic act became a quintessential moment of awakening for her and taught her invaluable lessons she would take with her and benefit from for the rest of her life. And what were those lessons? Enter the mysterious old sage in *Kai*.

Anne Marie spent the first ten years of her life in an orphanage on an island near Stockholm. One evening when she was alone in her bed in an attic storage room converted into her sleeping quarters, she had an encounter straight out of the twilight zone. As the moonlight beamed in through a window above her, she suddenly saw the figure of a man with long hair and darkish skin seated next to her. He seemed to be as light as air, for Anne Marie was sure the bed had no extra weight on it. The man's face was illuminated and smiling, and his gaze was at the same time comforting and frightening to the little girl. She peered at the strange apparition as long as she could and finally threw a blanket over her head when she could no longer contain herself. She never saw the mysterious presence again but would always remember him in a comforting way, and she would come to refer to him as her "Indian." Many years later, she saw a picture of her Indian over a mantle in a stately parlor room belonging to a professor she was studying and working with near San Diego. She was surprised to discover that her Indian had a name and a historical identity—but that is a story for another day.

Kai was written almost forty years ago. It is an altogether improbable and touching story, much like Anne Marie's life. Nearly everyone who has ever read the original manuscript has asked the author why she hasn't made the story into a book. After all this time, all we can say is: better late then never.

Ken Weiss
Idyllwild, California
July 2013

1

In a faraway corner of the world, neatly tucked away next to nowhere, was a small village called Zira. Here were people who lived, worked, and played just as people do in most any other village in the world.

The trees that surrounded Zira were really tall. They were so tall that the sky itself had to look up to them. And they grew so close together that, except for a few shady glens and meandering meadows, they stood like a solid wall against the outside world.

This slumbering little oasis of humanity would have passed in and out of history without ever so much as a yawn of notice were it not for Kai, a giant and ferocious snake who lived in the dense and dark forest that surrounded Zira on all sides.

Kai embodied all the worst attributes of the reptile kingdom, and his name was synonymous with terror and fear. The devilish serpent, whose body was as large as the trunk of a giant tree, and whose mind was more devious than ten villainous dragons, ruled his kingdom with a wicked and venomous nature. Kai was despicable, disgusting, and just about any other word you could think of that you would avoid at all cost and not even wish upon your worst enemy. He was a really bad dude.

Anyone who wanted to enter or leave Zira had only one option, a narrow sliver of a path barely wide enough for one person to walk on at a time. The trail was dark, treacherous, and menacing from start to finish. For this reason, some of the villagers never left Zira for the entirety of their lives, content to remain in the safety of the town rather than chance a surely deadly encounter with the evil Kai.

For those daring ones who were brave enough to defy death and test the Fates, there were rules that had to be followed in excruciating detail. For one thing, timing was everything. The villagers had to wait stoically until Kai's voracious appetite had been satiated on the flesh of some poor victim. When his belly was stuffed and bloated with prey, only then—when he had finally fallen asleep, after belching, and burping, and passing gas in a most disgusting manner—only then was it safe to attempt the crossing.

Even then there were enormous dangers to be faced. The villagers had to be ever so careful not to make a sound, hardly daring to breathe, lest the wretched beast be awakened and suddenly lash out at the doomed traveler in a fit of rage. It was understood by all that the villainous serpent did not have to be hungry to kill. Sport killing was second nature to this heartless monster.

The creatures of the forest fared even worse. All they could do when Kai appeared was scatter in all directions, run for their lives, and hope that someone less agile or alert would fall prey to his enormous and deadly jaws. Jaws like a black hole. When he opened his mouth to snatch a victim, his head and body seemed to split nearly in two. And to make matters even worse, venomous fangs flanked each side of that cavernous opening.

Kai's wicked mind and brute strength cast a dark shadow over all activities in and around Zira, and not even sleep brought relief from the abiding nightmare that stalked young and old day and night. No wonder the animals of the forest and the people of Zira lived in perpetual fear and felt for certain that their environs were cursed. Indeed, they were.

The stories of Kai were the main topic of conversation at every campfire and gathering. The lucky ones, those few who had succeeded in escaping the beast and making it through the forest alive, were always the center of attention. And the tales of their encounters with the cruel snake became increasingly horrific.

One told of having seen Kai swallow a mountain lion in a single gulp. Another spoke of how he had seen Kai wrap himself around a giant bear and squeeze him into a tiny ball of fur. But the real truth was that, in all likelihood, no one had ever seen Kai while the serpent was awake, for if they had, they would have never returned to the village to tell their tale.

Living under the constant and oppressive feeling of gloom and doom, the people of Zira adapted by becoming more closely knit as a group. In many ways they were like one large and brooding family, united in their fear, subdued under their collective curse, withdrawn and unremarkable. As a result, crime and violence were less likely to occur in Zira, and outside of some minor spats and disagreements, most lived together in a submissive and compliant sort of way. They went along to get along.

The only animals that seemed oblivious to the dreaded reptile were the birds. They perched in the trees and twittered, tweeted, and chirped above him all day, safe from his menacing glances and deadly reputation. This frustrated the snake to no end.

For hours at a time, he would lie on the ground, his head stretched upward, and watch in bewildered awe as these flighty creatures hopped from branch to branch or spread their wings and disappeared above the tall trees through an open hole in the sky to a place where he could not even imagine.

The notion that something existed, even thrived, within his kingdom and yet was outside his control was very unsettling to the serpent, bothering him for several reasons. Not being able to kill or devour everything was bad enough, but hearing their delightful songs and observing their playfulness and carefree existence inevitably started him thinking. Maybe, after all, there was something in life that he had been missing. It was true that he ruled the forest exactly as he pleased and that there was none who dared to challenge his authority. Still, after all the swaggering, the chasing, and the conquering, after the belly full of fresh prey and the long naps in the warm sun, what else was there to do but more of the same?

To the astute observer, it would appear that Kai was becoming a bit bored with his life.

2

One day, when Kai was resting under a rock and digesting a large mountain goat, he became aware of footsteps along the path close by. Instinctively, without even looking to see what it was, he lunged toward the sound and, in the blink of an eye, was wrapped around the body of his next victim. The beast teasingly raised his head to look at the poor creature that was but a squeeze, a bite, and a gulp away from a dastardly ending.

It was a human. But to Kai's great surprise, this one offered no resistance and only held himself still and relaxed under the serpent's iron grip. The old man's eyes were sympathetic, following the serpent's swaying head from side to side with keen interest and no fear.

Kai opened his mouth to bare his fangs closer to the face of his prey, but he got no more response than before. If anything, this human seemed amused. There was no cry of pain, not even the slightest twinge of alarm. In fact, he did not even breathe hard. Kai was taken aback. He was truly bewildered. Something was not right.

"What is wrong here?" he muttered out loud to himself.

Deprived and disgusted, he loosened his grip, and the man dropped to the ground. A genuine smile spread across the face of the stranger, and he opened his mouth to speak. "Good day, Kai, vicious beast of the forest!"

The stranger brushed his hands over his long white robe in an effort to smooth out the wrinkles Kai had caused, and he sat down on a rock beside him. "Good day, Kai," repeated the man, his voice friendly and kind.

Kai didn't answer, but out of the corner of his eye, he stole a glance at this unusual and foolish being. He was slight for a human and, dressed in his white robe, he gave the impression of being courteous and friendly.

In contrast to his small stature, the old man's face was framed by silvery hair and was sharp and distinctive. Even when smiling, it radiated a strange kind of power. The man's hands, still fussing with the robe, struck Kai the same way his face did, strong and firm, yet gentle and delicate.

Instinctively, Kai felt that this man sitting on the rock beside him was not just any ordinary villager trying some newfangled scheme to get by him, but instead, someone who deserved a closer look.

"Good day, Kai," the stranger repeated for the third time as he leaned closer.

Kai looked at the old man's eyes, and he saw that they were calm and deep, like the bottomless dark pools that existed in the most remote parts of the forest. "What's the matter with you?" the serpent wheezed. "Why aren't you afraid of me?"

An amused smile crossed the man's face. "Afraid of you, Kai? Surely you are joking. You, a confused snake destined to crawl around on your belly all your life. You must be kidding. Quite frankly, your kind is nothing to trouble oneself over, much less fear."

What an outrageous insult! Kai was beside himself. He was ready to lunge again, but a sudden curiosity about this strange intruder held him back. Even though he was bewildered, Kai was sure about one thing—this human had a lot of guts. In his whole life, no one had ever talked to him like that. "Destined to crawl around on my belly, am I?" he muttered. "Why should that matter?" But somehow, it did matter.

"Let me introduce myself," said the man on the rock. "My name is Esmir." Getting no response from Kai, he continued. "I am on my way to the village of Zira, but I thought I would seek you out first."

"Seek you out first," Kai repeated those words out loud to himself. Surely his ears were deceiving him. With everyone in this forest shuddering at the very thought of Kai's appearance, this defenseless and miserable fool had the gall to say that he wanted to seek him out. He must be crazy.

But Kai took the bait. "What for?" he snarled through his fangs, thumping his tail against the ground.

"Because I feel sorry for you," Esmir shot back, looking directly at the startled snake.

"You feel sorry for me?" Kai raised his powerful body up to its full length and, looking down menacingly on Esmir, he repeated again in stunned disbelief, "You feel sorry for me?"

Esmir ignored Kai's threatening posture and went on. "For years you have ruled the forest with your evil ways. You have wasted your life in senseless killings, and you have spawned fear and dread in all those you encountered. And what have you gotten in return for all the terror and chaos you've caused? Nothing, that's what—except your own vain self-glory." Kai, perhaps for the first time in his life, was dumbfounded and speechless.

"One day you will die, and there will be no reward for you anywhere. In that self-created hell to which you will go, you will continue to crawl on your belly for all eternity. Behind, you will leave not a single friend, nor any sign of mourning. Not one solitary tear will be shed at your passing. And you wonder why I feel sorry for you?"

Esmir waited patiently for Kai's answer, but since he was still too stunned to speak, the old man finally again continued. "I know that you are often lonely. I know, too, that at times you dream of being someone else, something less confining. Like some humans dream of bettering their lot in life, maybe you dream of becoming a light-footed deer or even a bird on the wing."

Esmir's words struck a sensitive chord in Kai's heart. The serpent was certain that he wasn't in pursuit of being anything better than he already was, for that was hardly possible. But, perhaps, for the additional power of controlling the sky the way he did the ground, and showing those birds a thing or two, for that Kai could dream a grander dream.

Without letting Esmir know how he really felt, he listened more intently. The old sage went on. "Creation is constantly adapting and refining itself. Everything that has a beginning also has an end, and every end is also a new beginning, and between these two polarities, life unfolds its destiny. Consider this, if you would. What adaptation is not possible? Could it be that what is not possible is only what we think to be not possible? I think so. You, Kai, can remain a villainous snake for as long as you wish, or you can retreat backwards into something even more despicable, although I don't suggest it."

Esmir's voice reached through the tangle of Kai's thoughts and was surprisingly soothing, like a haunting flute melody that captured his attention. "You can also choose to go forward and onward, however it is you deem that to be, and become a loftier expression of that aspiration. You want power, but you must eventually understand that you have chosen a very limited and short-lived way of getting it. Indeed you have."

Kai couldn't believe his ears, but he was spellbound nonetheless.

"The kind of power you possess is built on the fear you have caused all the helpless creatures who live in the forest, and this kind of power will only last as long as your body is strong, your fangs are filled with poison, and your mind is more agile than the prey you hunt. But, when all of that is no more, when old age and weariness set in, all the anguish you have caused others will return to you. You can be certain of that. What you sow, you eventually reap. It is the law of Nature. And then, Kai, you will be the chased, the persecuted, and the fearful fugitive, destined to die in the solitary hell of your own creating, undone by your own doing. Believe it, for it will most certainly come to pass."

Esmir stopped for a spell, searching Kai's face. It was pale and tortured. "If it is power you want," he went on, "there are better and nobler ways of getting it and keeping it."

"What kind of power are you talking about that I don't already have?" Kai was clearly shaken and had given up all pretenses of superiority and invulnerability.

"The power of self-control. The power to live and let live. The power that is greater than might makes right. The power that lies in the understanding of who you are, who you really are, beyond your limited belief of who you think you are. Do you understand? This is the only power that has any lasting value."

Esmir clearly had the upper hand now, and Kai knew it. "Okay! Okay!" Esmir's words were battering Kai's understanding of everything he thought he knew to be true, and he was struggling mightily to make sense of what he was hearing. "Let's pretend everything you say is true. How do you go about getting that kind of power? And suppose you got it, how do you know what to do with it?"

Esmir had waited for this moment. Kai was now, hopefully, ready to hear a radical new way of going about living. It would require a massive assault on the serpent's sensibilities, but Esmir was clearly up to the task.

"To begin with, you get it by being a source of harmony and cooperation in your everyday life, if you can ever imagine such a thing and stretch your mind around it. Stop with your hostilities. Stop scaring and killing all the creatures that lie around you, and start helping when you can, protecting when you are able, and showing kindness to all living beings that you meet."

Kai's response was predictable. "That's crazy! It's nonsense! How can you ever be so stupid to think that you will get more power by giving it up? That's the most stupid thing I have ever heard. It goes against everything that I've ever known to be true." And then, in a less sarcastic tone, "And even if it was true, I don't have a clue how to change who I am."

Esmir's task was now almost complete. Only a few more words needed to be spoken. "It is just as easy to affirm life as it is to negate it. And if you are really sincere in wanting to change, be assured you won't have to look for how to do it. Opportunities to practice goodness lie within every moment of life. You have the power to choose how you want your life to be. You'll see, if you only give yourself a fair chance."

The old man stood up and reached for his cane that was lying beside him. "Well, Kai, I must go now. Goodbye and good luck! I have no doubt that you will find yourself much happier and more contented with life if you change your ways. Haven't you felt the earth below your belly long enough? Isn't it time that you also gave yourself a chance to feel the sky above your head? Remember, that too is a part of the world in which you live, and as such, is also your rightful heritage."

With that, Esmir reached out in a parting gesture to lightly touch the serpent's head, but Kai instantly recoiled, his body ready to lunge. Nobody touched Kai. Nobody.

"I'll be thinking of you." Esmir turned and began walking away.

Kai watched him as he started down the narrow path. "Hey, wait a minute." Kai raced down beside him. "You still haven't told me how I will know when I have that kind of power you talk about."

Esmir turned to him and smiled. "You will know, Kai. You will know. You will feel it like warm sunlight flooding the inside of your magnificent self. It will bring a smile to your face, and at the same time, tears to your eyes. It will make you light as a leaf, yet as strong as the wind. You will feel as fluid as a stream and as still as the dawn."

The kind old man walked on, no longer aware of Kai's presence. In a clear and ringing voice, he began to sing as he continued down the path. "There is a land beyond this place, where dwells the One I love. It has no sun, nor moon, nor stars, yet radiates from above. A light so bright, so warm, so white, that words cannot convey. The sense of awe, beyond this pale, where all's made new each day. The land of my Beloved."

And then he was gone.

3

The encounter with Esmir seemed to leave no lasting impression on the unrepentant serpent. He continued to carry on in his usual caustic manner, terrorizing the forest, pursuing everything in sight, and devilishly enjoying himself every slither of the way.

Only one thing was different. Thinking of Esmir made Kai feel strangely uneasy. Why had he been so foolish as to let the intruder go free without ending his miserable life in a single gulp? Kai became angry at himself for such a dereliction of duty. "Never again," he vowed. "Never again."

Try as he might, he could not understand what had come over him, nor could he forgive himself for such a feeble and impotent response. "Imagine, I actually listened to him!" Kai blurted out one day while chasing a mountain lion that he happened upon, who had been taking a midday nap.

Over the rocks, under the bushes, around the trees, and across the hills—the wilder the chase, the more Kai thrilled in the pursuit. When he finally trapped the large cat on a steep ledge, he deftly wrapped his lower body around the frightened animal, thereby leaving it no place to jump except straight up into the air. Kai hovered here, his jaws wide open, his fangs bared, and his tongue split into two tense and quivering barbs ready to skewer the helpless prey.

The trap had been set masterfully, and now all that remained was for the steely serpent to look into the cat's eyes, which was usually enough to send his victim into a rigid paralysis, after which he only had to lower his head and close his jaws around the doomed quarry. With one last painful and bloodcurdling cry, the helpless cat surrendered to the snake's lusty urge and was quickly reduced to a huge lump in Kai's already bulging stomach.

"Not bad for a cat," Kai gloated with a loud and gross belch, slowly winding his way back to his favorite meadow. "In fact, for a cat, pretty darn good."

He stretched out on a log and closed his eyes, the better to feel the warm sun on his enormous body, now stuffed to nearly bursting. “Imagine, I actually listened to him.” Kai shook his head in disgust as the memory of Esmir once again unsettled his thinking. Just the thought of that old man was enough to give the snake a bad case of indigestion. Another belch, this one even louder and more disgusting, echoed out into the forest.

“He wasn’t much bigger than the skinny staff he carried, and yet I let him go. What was I thinking?” In his mind was crystallized a vivid picture of the slight stranger. The more he focused on the image, the more spellbinding and mysterious the white-robed man became. How strange that episode was becoming. It was almost like a hallucination that overtook and haunted him.

The way the old man talked was also very unsettling to Kai’s sense of propriety. “How could he possibly know anything about power?” Kai reasoned. “He’s nothing but a pathetic shadow of a man who didn’t have the strength to kill even a fly.”

The perplexed serpent stretched until his skeleton made the sound of crackling embers, and his body expanded and extended itself to nearly twice its normal length. "The only time you would have to resort to philosophizing about the kind of power that old man talked about was if you just plain didn't have it in your muscles and your own brain," Kai philosophized to himself. "But I, the great Kai, have plenty of brain power and mighty muscles. If my own mightiness doesn't make right, then what possibly could?"

Wasn't it true? Of course it was! A whip of his tail, a turn of his head, and a glaring glance was all it took to send the whole forest into shuddering palpitations. As for self-control, he certainly had more of that than anyone he'd ever met. Why, he could lie in wait for prey for hours on end without even so much as flicking an eyelid, no matter what was bothering him. And furthermore, he could stand up on his tail and hold himself as erect as a tree, a feat he had never seen anyone else come close to performing.

"About going to hell and all that bunk," he went on to himself, "the old man can go to hell. And besides, who really cares where you go after you've shed your last scales? Whatever made that vain and skinny poor excuse for a human think he had all the answers?"

However, there was one thing that the perplexed reptile had to admit. As much as he hated to own up to it, the white-robed wanderer was right about something. There was hardly any sense of challenge or adventure remaining in Kai's life. As of late, he had even thought about leaving the forest for happier hunting grounds farther away. It was true. Kai was beginning to tire of the sameness and the monotony of his life. A change, any change, would be most welcomed.

But how to do that? How does one become something other than what he is? Becoming a deer, or anything else for that matter, seemed like pure fantasy and nonsense. Besides, there was nothing he really admired about such a creature except, perhaps, that last mile of the chase. In its panic-stricken fear, the stag ran with a beauty and daring that Kai never ceased to envy. It could fling itself across crevices and obstacles with total abandon. Kai was amazed at how far it could go in such a short amount of time. Of course, Kai, in hot pursuit, was also traveling just as fast and overcoming the same obstacles, so whoever needed or wanted to be a deer? What was the point?

A bird on the wind—now that was a thing of a whole other feather. It was still nonsense, of course, but in some way, he could let himself embrace such a fantasy. To be able to lift himself above the gravity of the earth and sweep across the sky over the tops of the trees and mountains . . . that was something he could dream about. Yes indeed!

In fact, in a strange way that he couldn't really understand, the hunger in his heart for such an experience was becoming something of an obsession, and almost more than he could bear. How many times had he found himself lost in a daydream, with his eyes closed and his mind focused on the sky? If he slowed his breathing in just the right way, he could imagine himself lifting off, taking flight, terrorizing the bird population, and exploring the wide-open spaces of the wild blue yonder above him. He could even look down and see where he had been.

What great fun it was! He could sense the air rush to meet his open wings, and they would spread so wide, and thrust with such power, up and down and up and down, as he heard the swoosh of air passing through his feathers, and he felt the lift and acceleration, as he watched the landscape unfold below, until he was absolutely caught in the revelry of the moment. He was now conquering the sky as he had conquered the earth. For a fleeting moment, his most fervent dream was almost a reality. His heart was pounding, his adrenaline flowing, and vivid imagery was overtaking his senses. Was he really flying?

Then suddenly, in an inexplicable way and with a bewildering sigh, a loud belch, and a hard thump, he was right back on his log, and he was in his old bulky and lumbering body again, with yet another big meal gurgling in his gut and needing to be digested.

Kai fought the disappointment and the desire to sleep. He could not get Esmir out of his mind. What had the old man implied that now haunted and stupefied the snake? "Nothing is beyond our reach! And whatever we think, we can be, if we are willing to persevere and let go." Could it really be true?

Thinking back through all those years, as far back as his mind could remember, it certainly had been so in Kai's life, at least until now. There had never been anything that he could not get either by bite, by brawn, or by brain. Absolutely nothing . . . until he began observing those pesky birds, whose presence had become a constant reminder that there was something else to life above and beyond his own world. Even so, how could he hope to achieve the impossible? Without wings, how could he soar through the sky the way the birds did?

Besides, even if he could grow them, they would have to be smooth enough to be folded close to his body and not interfere with him getting around on the ground. Flying was one thing, but he was not about to be hopping on a pair of spindly legs, especially not when he was able to slither so swiftly through hills, valleys, and dales the way he could.

Just the same, to prove that he could fly like a bird, if only for a little while, would satisfy his most fervent dream and would be a feat no other snake had ever done. And it would certainly take him out of his doldrums. If in trying there would be even a remote chance that Esmir was right, the whole experiment would surely be worth it. What did he have to lose?

Kai pondered the possibilities with one eye open, following a bumblebee that had seen fit to distract him for the moment. He was too engrossed in his thoughts and too lazy to brush it away. But when the bee took a close dive across his face and nearly brushed his nose before finally buzzing out of earshot, Kai droned out loud, "Even a dumb thing like that can fly." Then he mumbled more softly, "So why can't I?"

How to go about doing it, though? That was the problem. He tried to remember what Esmir had said.

Something about being kind to all living things, and helping, and protecting, and being a source of good. What was that all about? Was he really serious?

Did it mean that he had to stop chasing and killing all that delicious prey that had been put in the forest for his personal pleasure and culinary enjoyment? Heaven forbid! And what about those horrible humans? Wouldn't he have to avoid them too? They were noisy and disgusting. They didn't smell good either. Even if they slipped by his watchful eye, he could trace their peculiar odor for miles. Kai despised humans most of all. They were like a plague to everyone in the forest. Everyone! These wretched beings, with few exceptions, cut down the trees, fouled the earth, and even killed some of the wildlife that ought to be reserved for him alone.

The memory of the stranger again pressed itself across his mind. Kai was still trying to understand what made this old guy that he had almost devoured so different from the rest. For one thing, he didn't smell or look like any of the others. It wasn't the robe he wore or the stick he carried or his long silver hair that made him so different.

Maybe it was the feeling he exuded, like the insistent whistling of the wind through the forest or the steady push of an underground spring. It was more of an invisible than visible thing. It bespoke of quiet strength and harnessed power. "Controlled power," Kai spoke the words slowly. "That was it! Power that was harnessed and at the same time still wild and free."

Suddenly Kai was wide awake. He moved gracefully off his log and into the shade of an old oak tree. Esmir was a conduit for that kind of power. That's the power Kai had felt when he was confronted by the old man in their first meeting. That's what haunted him to this day. What was it he had called it? "The power of self-control!" Yeah, that was it.

"The power of self-control," Kai repeated the words slowly and deliberately. "If I could get that kind of power along with what I already have, I'd really be something. I could be the king of everything, the king of the whole world instead of just this forest. Even Esmir would have to bow to me. Of that I would make certain."

Kai stretched his thoughts until his head felt like an expanding balloon that was ready to burst from overinflation. He could sense the sudden welling of inspiration turn into a resolve that he would undertake immediately.

Very well! He would try to get the kind of power that Esmir exhibited, even if the method of acquiring it seemed strange and silly. He would let those scared animals and those wicked people have a chance to get around freely for a while. He would keep to himself and only give chase and kill when he was hungry and needed to eat. After all, being good couldn't possibly mean that he would have to stop eating altogether. Kai was sure Esmir couldn't have meant that killing for his survival was excluded from the plan he was about to undertake. "I'll give it a go. What have I got to lose?"

It wouldn't be easy. The part about giving up killing just for the pleasure of killing would be hard enough. But the idea of helping and protecting, which Esmir had also told him to practice, was incomprehensible and totally out of the question.

"Let them help themselves," Kai sneered as he coiled his body into a series of perfect concentric circles. "Nobody ever cared about me, and I am not about to run around the forest looking for somebody who needs help. No way. That would only create weaklings and cause lots of dependency." The last thing he needed was anyone dependent on him. What if they got used to him helping them and suddenly he decided to call off the crazy experiment? All the thrill and challenge of chasing would be gone. Without that, he might as well give up living altogether.

Kai spent the rest of the day and evening concentrating on how he would best adapt to this change in his life. He crawled back to his rock later than usual, quite pleased with himself, and with a clear idea of how he would implement his new resolve.

4

It was not long before the animals in the forest, as well as the people of Zira, began to realize that the curse of Kai had been lifted. Their lives were no longer in danger. Cautiously at first, they began to penetrate deeper into the forest that for so long had been Kai's exclusive domain. Aside from a few rustlings in the dense foliage or a few rumblings of loose rocks falling in the distance, there were no more indications that Kai was still around or even alive.

No one could understand what had happened to the feared serpent. One rumor had it that he was ill and dying a slow death. Another, that he had been attacked by a pack of ferocious wolves and had been nearly beaten to death. Then there was the village seer, who said that she had seen Kai in a dream and that he had been struck by lightning and was now completely blind.

A few of the villagers were certain that Esmir, the ascetic who had recently moved to the village, had exorcised Kai and removed the age-old curse that the serpent had held over their lives. They reasoned that this mysterious stranger, who now lived on the outskirts of their village, must have passed through the forest initially and encountered the vile beast. Although no one dared question Esmir about it, among themselves they concluded that he must have somehow vanquished the serpent and not made any mention of it to them.

Esmir was a strange soul, if there ever was one. His behavior mystified these simple village people to no end. He had made his home in a small hut on the edge of the village, where he could be seen studiously tending his garden or sitting quietly for hours on end in silent meditation, smiling softly with his face toward the sun. He always had a gentle aura about him and a subtle air of contentment that spilled over into his surroundings.

Only on rare occasions, when Esmir would venture to the marketplace to buy some needed staples, did the people of Zira have the opportunity to interact with this humble man. Aloof and yet friendly, he made his way through the market's stands and stalls, selecting fruits, vegetables, herbs, and grains and exchanging a few words of greeting with the vendors and nearby shoppers. Then, placing his goods into a woven sack he carried over his shoulder, he headed for the large fountain in the middle of the town.

Lingering next to this pool, Zira's most distinguishable landmark and its central meeting place, he would quietly sit and begin peeling a piece of fruit

with the casual ease of a person who had all the time in the world to enjoy and reflect on his surroundings.

Slowly and deliberately, one bite at a time, he would nibble on the fruit. Anyone watching him couldn't help but feel that he was enjoying himself immensely and that he was relishing every last sensation of sweetness and flavor that the tasty morsels offered up to him, in total delight. He would take each seed from the fruit, rub it clean between his fingers, and then place it ever so carefully into a sachet, and then into his knapsack.

After he finished eating, he would sit serenely and gaze upon the scene about him, offering in his own unique way a quiet invitation for people to join him. Some of them did, but no one ever engaged him, yet neither did any of them ridicule him because of his strange appearance and mannerisms. His presence commanded respect.

After a while, he would stand up and take leave, never failing to raise his hand and smile in a friendly gesture, to which they all nodded. Then they would watch him as he turned and walked away, until he had disappeared over the hill. Afterward, they would get together in small groups, trying to figure out who he was and why he had come to stay so close to Zira. More and more, they grew to accept him for who and what he was, without knowing who or what he was, and they actually began to love the old man for the new sense of security that he brought to their community.

Yes, he was an enigma. But if he had anything to do with the disappearance of Kai, he was certainly their friend.

5

Time passed. With the threat of Kai gone from their lives, the fear that had united the people for so long was also gone. They began unleashing some of their restraints and expressing more of the frustrations they had harbored over the years. As a result, dissension and turmoil began to spread, and Zira was even gloomier than before.

The news of Kai's fate became especially significant for the children, who had always been told frightful stories about the serpent and warned about how important it was that they behave, or else the villainous beast would come and eat them. Now, instead of Kai pursuing them, they wanted to get after him.

One morning, young and old alike gathered together in the town square, and armed with sticks and pitchforks, they set out in force to find the snake and kill him, if he was still alive. The bullies and ruffians, who were actually the most cowardly in the group, led the way, with the children close behind. Soon, the whole lot of them was stomping their way into the depths of the forest. There was anger, cursing, and confusion everywhere. Finally, late in the afternoon, one of the older children happened upon Kai and screamed, "I see him! He's over here! He's over here! Come quick! Let's get him!"

Kai had been napping under the canopy of a black oak tree. He was still a bit groggy as his peaceful state was rudely interrupted by the sight of dozens of villagers rushing at him with hate and evil intentions. What to do? He immediately began to muster up all the discipline and self-control that he had so painstakingly gained through the months of working to harness his wild and savage instincts. His body stiffened as he raised his head to glare at the murderous group that now encircled him.

The shouting only grew louder. After the initial fear and shock at seeing the huge snake had subsided, one of the men yelled in a shrill voice, “Come on, let’s kill him!” Soon everyone took up the chant, “Kai must die! Kai must die!”

When the first rock hit Kai’s head, it stunned him. No one in all the forest had ever dared to challenge him, much less attack his formidable body. Before he could get over the first rock’s impact, another heavy stone struck him, which was followed by a barrage of blows on his unprotected body. So far, it had been fairly easy to follow Esmir’s advice of nonviolence, since none of the creatures in the forest had ever bothered him. But this unforeseen brutal attack on his privacy, on his nonviolent practices, and quite possibly on his life was totally incomprehensible.

He writhed in agony and struggled under the merciless hits of his attackers. A stabbing and stinging pain racked his body, and he saw through his blood-spattered eyes the prongs of a pitchfork piercing into him, and then another and another. Whipping his tail with a mighty jerk, he managed to free himself from the hostile mob, and he watched how his attackers fell back at this sudden movement and the unexpected sight of his huge body thrashing its way out of their savage reach.

Kai was badly hurt. His body left a trail of blood as he managed, with his last ounce of strength, to reach the safety of his home under the rock. There, in the cool darkness and protection of this impregnable fortress, not one of his attackers dared follow. With their clamorous voices fading into the distance, Kai fell into merciful unconsciousness.

"He's dead! He's dead! The beast is dead!" The children and town folks jubilantly sang their victory cry and ran back to Zira to tell of how they had cornered and fought the ferocious serpent and how they watched him, mortally wounded, slither away from them and disappear.

Esmir soon learned of Kai's fate. He immediately set out to find the truth for himself. It was pitch dark when he reached the forest, but he walked with the same decisiveness and ease of step to the spot where Kai had been attacked as if it were broad daylight. Then he followed the blood-stained trail back to Kai's rock.

Through a haze of anguish and pain, the wounded serpent slowly became aware of Esmir's voice. "Kai, where are you? Kai?" Esmir was filled with concern as he leaned down under the rock to where Kai lay. Though he tried to answer, Kai couldn't make a sound. His throat was parched, his body racked with pain, and all he wanted was to be left alone to die. Esmir continued, "Kai, let me help you."

With a great effort, he finally managed to drag himself out into the open. He felt Esmir's hand touch his body, and the old man poured cool water down his throat. "Thank heaven you are alive! What a terrible mess they have made of you." The old man's voice was firm and tinged with anger.

He carefully scrutinized the deep cuts on Kai's blood-encrusted body. Esmir washed them clean and quickly gathered some plants from the nearby meadow. He squeezed the herbs through his fingers and allowed the healing sap to drip into Kai's open wounds. From a spring he fetched wet clay, which he then spread over Kai's entire body until he looked like a muddied lump of earth.

The wounded serpent was weakly aware of what Esmir was doing. However, he had the strength to neither resist nor follow what was going on. Instead, he let himself again sink deeply into that dark well of oblivion, where time and suffering have no room to abide. He closed his eyes and was gone.

Kai had no idea how long he had been dead to the world. When he finally returned to consciousness, the first thing he saw was Esmir's face with a broad smile on it. "Welcome back, dear friend! Welcome back, noble king of the forest!"

"What happened?" Kai made a move to shift his weight and noticed that although he was very stiff, the pain was gone.

"Well, you got some of your own medicine, and you took it very well."

Kai lay still, trying to recall what had happened. Beyond the screaming of the children and the stabbing pain of the pitchforks, he had no recollection whatsoever.

"You were really badly cut up," Esmir responded, as if reading Kai's thoughts. "It's a moon later, and now you have had a most beautiful healing sleep. Whatever you suffered in the past is now only a distant memory." Stroking Kai's head, the old man continued. "And you are now as good as new, or maybe even better."

Kai trembled slightly. In all of his life, no one had ever touched him, yet Esmir's hand on his head filled him with soothing warmth. He remembered their last meeting, when the old man had reached out to pat him and he had recoiled, wanting to strike back. At this moment, it seemed so very long ago.

In some inexplicable way, he had a feeling he was no longer the same individual he had been—but someone altogether different. But who was he? The only thing he knew for sure was that he wasn't quite sure of anything anymore. How good it would be if he could figure it all out.

6

The sun was radiating through the forest canopy, and its warmth felt good on Kai's body. He stretched out to his full, magnificent length and reveled in the joy of being alive and knowing that Esmir was near him. As he lay there relaxed and grateful, he became aware of an enthralling sound that filled the air. The giant snake looked up, and there was Esmir sitting on the top of a rock, eyes closed, flute in hand, his body swaying from side to side.

Kai was transfixed at the sight and sound, watching and listening as the soothing music reverberated through the forest countryside, coaxing every cell and nerve of his body into a heightened awareness. Instinctively, he raised himself up and began to sway in unison with Esmir's movements, feeling the tranquil waves slowly but surely overtake his senses and ripple across his outstretched form. Before he knew it, he was floating on wings of sound, entranced in currents of euphoria. He pitched and rolled back and forth, not really in his body, and not really in his mind. Did that mean he was out of his body, or just out of his mind? Who knew for sure?

When the music finally stopped, the silence hit him like a stone wall. In the stillness of that reverberating moment, when he finally opened his eyes, he saw Esmir watching him and smiling. "Where were you, Kai?" His voice was warm and friendly but had a teasing undertone to it.

"I don't know," the snake replied. "I can't really remember. I must have dozed off." He furrowed his brow in a futile gesture. "It felt a little weird," he added, hesitant and embarrassed to tell Esmir what he'd really experienced.

The wise one in the white robe abruptly changed the subject. He looked intently at Kai. "Why did you allow the people of Zira to attack you the way they did?"

Kai couldn't believe his ears. A burning fury swept through the whole of his body, compounded by the many months of suppressing his real, primordial nature. Quick as lightning, the snake lashed out at the old man. “You should ask such a stupid question? It’s because of your idiotic and dangerous philosophical platitudes that I allowed them to attack me as they did.”

The serpent was so incensed that he could barely speak. His breathing became agitated, his heart pounded, and his eyes clouded over in a storm of rage. “How dare you say this to me now,” he roared. “For months I did everything you asked of me. I crawled around like a scared worm. I bothered no one, even as my privacy was invaded and my pride crushed by lowly and pathetic humans. And all for what? What was the point of it all? And now, after I have suffered the ultimate humiliation that almost killed me, you have the audacity to ask me why I allowed it?”

Kai was now beside himself with rage. His words thundered through the forest and bellowed out at the old man in utter disdain. “Thanks to you, I was but a final blow from being killed, and yet I did not retaliate. I let your stupid words overshadow my good sense when I should have killed them all. Now you dare question me and, worse yet, make your question sound like an accusation!”

The resurrected beast inside Kai jerked up and swept his head menacingly before Esmir's face. His tail banged against the ground, and he was furious enough to grab the old man and cut him in two with a single swipe.

"Easy, easy," Esmir's voice rang cool and clear on Kai's enraged senses. "It is true that I told you to stop chasing and killing, but I never told you not to defend yourself when your life was at stake, did I?"

"Well," the snake snarled, "if that is true, the only way I know how to defend myself is to kill rather than be killed. Since you seem to have all the answers, tell me how else I could have defended myself?"

"All you had to do was hiss."

Kai let Esmir's words sink into his mind as he struggled to understand what he meant.

"All you had to do was hiss," the old man repeated.

"Mr. wise guy," Kai snorted. "I never threaten without hissing, and I never hiss without striking, and I never strike without killing!"

"You mean you never did," Esmir interjected.

"I mean I never do!" Kai shot back.

"Well then, why not try it? It saves a great deal of work and a lot of pain."

Kai lowered himself to the ground. He was sullen and morose, tired of arguing. It didn't really matter anyway. In that moment, he only wished that Esmir would be out of his life. It would have been better had they never met. He thought how nice it would be to go back to his old life and be his big, bad self again. After all, what had he gained for all his efforts? Absolutely nothing, except an encounter with a near-death experience.

For one thing, he certainly hadn't come an iota closer to becoming a bird, and after all, as stupid as it sounded, that's what this had all been about. He shook his body impatiently in an attempt to retrieve some of those vile and devilish feelings that once had been so much a part of him. How he would love to, once more, race through the forest and strike at everything in sight, and wound, and kill, and devour to his heart's content until he had his fill. And he would never have his fill.

He would start with Esmir. He'd just take that white-robed good-for-nothing phony, toss him up in the air, and let him bounce around for a while. That had been one of his favorite games and best tricks, throwing his prey up in the air. Then, fast as a blink, he would tighten his body to act as a spring so he could yo-yo his victim up and down until the meat got good and soft. Only then—and his mouth drooled at the very thought of it—only then was the stage properly prepared for the kill!

Out of the corner of one eye, he stole a sly look at Esmir. Seeing the old man sitting there so defenseless yet so calm and utterly unperturbed, Kai knew he could never do it. As a matter of fact, Kai was quite sure that he could never again get any real pleasure out of chasing and hunting anything for sport.

The serpent was in a quandary. His mind was very confused and very depressed. “Perhaps,” he thought, “I have lost my courage.” To be a snake and not be able to act like one was bad enough, but to be a gutless snake . . . that would be worse than death.

Still, something had begun to happen to him that was totally unlike his old self. He recalled an incident that had occurred a short time ago. He had been crossing one of the meadows in the forest and had surprised a young doe grazing in the tall grass. There he was, only a leap away from her—he could have easily wrapped himself around the defenseless creature’s legs and finished her in a heartbeat.

But he didn't.

He raised his head and got a full view of the startled deer. Quick as the wind, she took off for the bushes. When the doe realized she was not being pursued, she stopped and turned. As their eyes met across the meadow, Kai suddenly experienced a strange sense of power—not because he could have easily killed her but because he had the strength to resist this impulse and had spared her.

Of late, there had been several occasions like that, and they had all been partially responsible for the change in Kai's behavior. That was why he knew he could never again return to his former way of life, no matter how much he might have wished for it to be otherwise.

Esmir had quietly slipped away to search for some food from a nearby fruit tree. When he returned, Kai looked up. "Try to get some nourishment," Esmir gently urged his friend. "A snake like you can't live on ruminations and cogitations alone."

They ate in silence, and Kai had to admit that he enjoyed the fruit as well as the comfort and warmth of Esmir's presence. After the meal was finished, they rambled together through the forest. There was Kai, gliding and turning his immense body in graceful and undulating moves, with Esmir striding right beside him. The agile serpent was surprised that there was no more pain anywhere. The time of rest had done wonders for him. As a matter of fact, he felt better than he ever had before.

He slid through the grass and over the rocks with ease. When they reached one of the many lakes, he swiftly cut across the cool water, leaving the old man far behind. Kai plunged toward the black bottom of the huge lake, diving deeper and deeper, and shot up again in a cascade of frothy spray. Breaking the surface, he whipped his body from side to side and watched as rippling wavelets were launched outward, where they rushed to the shore in gentle, concentric rings.

He turned over and floated like a still log on his back, gazing at the sky above. With no trees to block his view, he watched in fascination as fleecy clouds rolled across the blue horizon and disappeared behind a giant green curtain. He saw Esmir perched on a rock high above, looking down at him with keen interest. It felt good to see him sitting there.

In fact, it felt very good just to be alive.

7

For Kai, the times that followed all blended into a beautiful tapestry, a weave of lighthearted and relaxed harmony with his surroundings. Never before had he felt the pulse-beat of life with such intensity and utter contentment. Slowly, and with the same care that one gives the most delicate of flowers, Esmir guided Kai's thinking farther and farther away from his old habits and closer to the path that leads to rebirth and renewal.

"Without a dream," Esmir would tell him, "you are nothing but a leaf in the wind, tossed and blown without intent or direction, and with little chance to find any purpose or calling. You are merely stuck in your past. If you do not unfold your possibilities in a conscious way in the present, how can there be anything better for you in your future?"

"What guarantee do any of us have that there is anything beyond what we are right now?" Kai asked.

Esmir was pleased whenever Kai made an effort to understand something over and above the ken of his awareness. "I wouldn't call it a guarantee. It's more like a covenant that you make with yourself. It's the sincerity of the commitment that will clear the way for you and ensure the outcome. A long time ago, I traveled the road you are on now. What you are today is my yesterday, and I am today what you can be tomorrow. That's how I know."

"Are you trying to tell me that you were once a snake?" Kai hid an impulse to laugh out loud.

"Not necessarily," Esmir reflected. "Frankly, I will admit to you that if I ever was, I don't remember. But one thing I do know for certain: what I am now is but the sum total of all I have been before. For example, look at this body I presently occupy. Its expression stands in direct relation to the requirement of the mind that inhabits it. My mind did not always have the need to create and perform the way it does now. When these talents were nothing more than budding potentials, I did not require a body with the kind of refinement that I now possess."

Kai looked at Esmir, whose hands were busily twining a mat out of the tall grass. He followed the delicate movements of his fingers, mesmerized by what he saw. "Only fingers," he thought, and yet each of them seemed to perform the very same movements as did his own body, only in a much more detailed way.

"Something doesn't make sense. If what you say is true, then how would it be possible for you and I to be communicating in this way? Aren't we discussing matters that lie far beyond the possible comprehension of what is usually evidenced by those who occupy a snake body like I now occupy?" Kai moved his tail from side to side as he pondered his own question.

"Because you are different. What you seem to be today is not what you really are, but rather, something that you were long ago." The old man hesitated. "Somewhere along your journey, you misused your power. Better said, you became intoxicated with your power, and therefore you lost the need for a more refined and complex body to express yourself through. You retreated into the simpler form you now have and became stuck in it, even as you continued to crave more power and domination over others. Consequently, you grew larger and more ferocious until you arrived at being the biggest and baddest snake in all creation.

"Still, you retain a distant memory of being a more advanced life form, and that is why you are not like any ordinary snake. The sense of boredom you have felt of late is a very positive sign. It means you have used up the need to remain what you've been and you are now ready for change."

Kai looked perplexed, but Esmir continued. "The beauty of creation is its constant adaptation to our ever-changing lives as we develop from the simple to the more complex. Creation creates evolution, and evolution evolves creation. Never think of them as separate from each other. They're partners. And that is why there are so many millions of different life forms in the world. They are all connected, for they all carry the same knowledge from a common source inside them, even if it has been covered over and forgotten."

"How am I supposed to believe all that?" The serpent was a bit agitated and had a hard time holding back a snarl of contempt.

Esmir looked at him and smiled. "It isn't really important what you and I believe. In fact, I sincerely suggest that you do not believe anything I say. Just keep this in mind: you are a snake, aren't you?"

"Yes, and I'm proud of it."

"Well then, just ponder what is happening inside of you. Why do you want to be something else than who and what you are? Stay a snake and be happy with it." Kai didn't have an answer, so the old man continued. "Perhaps you want to become something else because you are already becoming something else. The experiencing and imagining essence of who you truly are has already felt the loftiness of a bird, the swiftness of a deer, and even the complexities of being a human."

Esmir paused to give Kai a chance to reflect. "Go on, go on. I'm listening. You've got my attention," Kai had to admit.

"No, one day you will know it by yourself, and I don't want to deprive you of that moment by giving parts of it now, which would only confuse you. Besides, I'm hungry. Why don't you get us some of those ripe cherimoyas that are ready to drop from the tree over there? What do you say?"

Esmir gave Kai a gentle nudge, and in one thrust, the athletic snake was wrapped around a slender tree trunk, his upper body carefully stretching out toward the fruit-laden branches. As deft as he was strong, he maneuvered himself between the tiny branches until he could clasp the fruit in his jaws. He tossed them delicately, one by one, into the old man's lap.

Before climbing back to the ground, he also dropped several of the light-green, oddly shaped fruit down for himself. Even though things that grew on trees and bushes were not his favorite foods, he had learned to stomach them on Esmir's advice. Freshly caught prey that still trembled with life was his real pleasure, but since being with the old man, he had consented to include in his diet such things as roots, fruits, and even certain herbs and grains. Strangely enough, he hadn't lost any of his strength. If anything, he felt better than ever, and certainly not as sluggish as he used to be after consuming a big meal of fresh flesh.

Kai slid back down the tree and slipped with graceful ease past Esmir. The fading light of dusk gave a soft blush to his undulating body, as it effortlessly moved down the path in a regal and statuesque manner. The great serpent ruler of the forest of Zira, the imposing and awesome Kai, was becoming even more impressive in his advancing years. For now, he was not only a physical marvel and a force of nature, but he also radiated an aura of sublime dignity, nobility, and virtue.

Without a doubt, Kai was becoming the most magnificent snake in all of creation.

8

One day Esmir was gone.

Kai had slept longer than usual. When he came out from under his rock, he was surprised to see that the sun was already flooding his meadow. It took him a few seconds to realize that the soothing call of Esmir's flute had failed to awaken him. He looked at the vacated rock from which the old man had been greeting him every morning, and suddenly he felt alone. Each and every morning, since the day Esmir had come to tend Kai's wounds, the old man had been sitting there on his mat, playing his flute, and gently swaying from side to side, connected to an inner sense of self that was both mysterious and enchanting. Kai had come to treasure those melodies and those moments.

He raised his body to its full length and looked for any sign of Esmir. All that was left on the rock was the little grass mat that he had woven when he first came. His only other possessions—his robe, his staff, and his sack—were no longer there.

Kai sadly lowered himself back to the ground. "He couldn't have gone too far." His eyes turned in every direction, and his ears listened for the sound of footsteps, but there were none to be heard. He slipped through the grass and across the meadow, toward the path that he and the old man had traveled so many times. "Esmir! Esmir!" he called again and again, but only the echo of his anguished cries came back through the heavy forest mist.

Instinctively, he felt it was useless to go on, for he was sure that Esmir had left the forest and that he would not be back again, at least not for a while. He circled around and around, going nowhere, but with a nervous need to be doing something, if only to keep moving. The pain of separation and loss was already gripping at his heart.

Here was self-reliant and independent Kai, who had had no need for anyone and no feelings for any other living beings except contempt, now torn with an inconsolable longing for someone who was not even of his own kind.

"Bull!" he raged.

In a fury, he whipped his tail back and forth on the rocky ground, and the earth shook with disapproval. Next, he stormed across the lake in a wild frenzy, making the water churn and froth violently, and creating a small tsunami in the process, but all to no avail.

"Bull!" he screamed again, even louder this time.

Finally, utterly exhausted and despondent, and with no desire to do anything more, he returned to his lonely rock. He turned his body into a huge coil, buried his head in the middle of it, and brooded on his miserable fate.

After a long silence, he thundered to no one in particular, "I was able to make it before I met him, and I can certainly make it again!" With that, he took a deep breath and then let loose a deeper sigh, and finally the serpent fell into a troubled sleep.

The days turned into weeks, and the weeks into months. Seasons passed, time marched on, and the waxing and waning of the forest's natural rhythms once more helped bring Kai out of himself. He was becoming accustomed to being alone again. Deep inside, he cherished the hope of someday seeing Esmir—somehow, somewhere, sometime. But meanwhile, there were things to do.

Kai was busier than ever. With a more focused attitude, the revitalized serpent moved through his forest with a new sense of purpose, observing and discovering things that before he had overlooked or deemed as unimportant.

Esmir had given him the key to removing his blinders and seeing things in a new and fascinating light. Kai was no longer exclusively bound by the norms and routines of his own conditioning but was now the principal participant and actor on the ever-changing stage that was his life. There was no more time to be bored. Life was a kaleidoscope of wonder, and he didn't want to miss any of it—with only one exception.

He had no interest, whatsoever, in the comings and goings of the inhabitants of Zira. He could forgive, but not forget, what they had done to him, and he always kept them at a respectable distance. Truth be known, he felt mostly sadness and sympathy for this confused breed of animals that called themselves humans. For the most part, they were an altogether sorry species.

True to his new philosophy, he no longer attacked or troubled anyone. But if the villagers dared to take even one step across the territory that Kai claimed as his own, he stood like a mighty wall, his chest wide, his mouth open, and his fangs glaring, as if to say, "I dare you." And if it was ever necessary to issue his horrifying hiss, veritable fire came out of his breath, and the people retreated in dread, never to be seen again.

Those who had thought Kai dead now believed that this was the reincarnation of the dreaded beast, returned with even more power and ferociousness than the one they thought had been killed. It was a bad omen, as the village soothsayers reminded everyone. Zira would be forever cursed. The villagers resigned themselves to this reality and again became fearful and submissive citizens. How strange they were. More than anything, Kai pitied them.

The animals in the wilderness still had some apprehensions regarding the great serpent, but these were now colored with a measure of respect. More than anything, it was the humans they feared as their main adversary. As a result, they gravitated to the safety and protection that the snake afforded them. And Kai, who was ever becoming more sensitive to his surroundings, could not help but feel their increasing trust and acceptance of him. The noble overseer began to relish the idea of being a steward of the forest, and he grew to enjoy the occasional demands this calling required of him.

He remembered what Esmir had once told him. "It is coping with life's challenges that makes you what you are."

They had happened upon a little scrub of a tree that was trying, against all odds, to eke an existence out of a small crevice in a giant rock. Planted firmly in the rich soil next to the rock stood another tree of the same family, but this one was tall, healthy, and stalwart, its roots receiving ample nourishment and its branches extending skyward and feeding on the warm sunlight.

Esmir had keenly studied the two of them for many moments. "You know, they were seeds born out of the same cone, but one fell onto the good earth that nurtured its growth while the other fell into unfriendly and hostile surroundings, where it had to struggle just to stay alive. Look at the difference."

Kai nodded in agreement.

"I believe," continued the old sage, "that if we replanted that spindly tree in the same soil as its twin, it would shoot to the stars in a burst of newfound desire to fulfill its potential. Its life force, that had been used only for surviving, would now be free and would unfold magnificently."

Kai found himself pondering so many of Esmir's wonderful utterances. And, more and more, he let his own wondering ways guide him into worlds he had never before considered or explored.

9

It was one of those lazy moments in early spring. Warmed by a returning sun, much appreciated after a long and blustery winter, Kai was resting on the edge of his favorite meadow. Diverted by a rustling in the tree above him, he looked up just as a tiny bird was falling to the ground. It landed with a hard thump, and though the startled serpent couldn't see it anymore, he was sure it was dead.

He made his way toward the site of the mishap and found the bird wedged within a small cavity inside a narrow crevice that nearly split an upright boulder in two. To his surprise and amazement, the tiny bird was still alive. He could see its frightened eyes blinking wildly and clinging to the will to live.

A genuine desire to save this teeny little one overtook the concerned Kai, and he quickly surmised the scene and weighed his next course of action. The split in the giant rock was too narrow, and the bird had plunged too deeply into the crack to be freed. Even if he could get to the bird, which he couldn't, he would only push it farther into its granite tomb. The crevice had saved the bird by lessening the impact of the fall, but unless Kai could do something, and do it quickly, the bird would die anyway.

Kai surveyed the scene from all angles. He noticed that the rock was actually split all the way to the bottom, and there was a hollow space underneath that he might be able to access. Ever so slowly, he forced his head and neck into the tight space and began pressing upward. It was agonizing work, and he wondered if he would also get stuck in the rock and meet with a similar fate as the bird above him. But he pushed on, beyond the panic and pain of the moment, until he felt the top of his head touch the bird's trembling body. Then, with even more resolve, ever so carefully, he nudged himself farther up into the crack above him, willing his body to contract even more, and guiding the wounded bird ever upward. When he could push no further, with a final desperate heave of his forehead, he gave a thunderous cry, like that of a warrior who had given his all and was now triumphant, no matter what the outcome.

His head and neck throbbed with a cutting pain that almost caused him to black out. The sensitive scales and skin of his forehead and brow were badly scraped, and blood streamed into his nostrils and eyes, nearly blinding him, as he slowly descended back down the inside of the rock. Finally, he managed to free himself from his granite containment, and he cautiously made his way around and back to the top of the rock.

There was the bird . . . out of the abyss . . . on its back . . . unable to move . . . badly wounded . . . but breathing. Unbelievable!

"What a pitiful little thing you are," Kai muttered, and just then, seeing the serpent, the bird made a feeble attempt to get away.

"Where do you think you're going?" Kai opened his jaws and scooped up the bird, doing his utmost not to hurt the tiny creature. He could feel its fluttering heartbeat pulsate against his palate, and for a fleeting instant, the temptation to bite down and swallow overtook him. Resisting the primitive impulse, he laid the bird as gently as he could on the soft leaves below the tree from which it had fallen. It made another piddling effort to move, but apparently both of its wings were broken, for they hung limply at its side.

Kai was at a loss as to what to do next. After all, how could a clumsy snake aid something as delicate and fragile as a wounded little bird? "If only Esmir was here," he thought out loud. "He would for certain know what to do."

Thinking of his friend suddenly brought back the vivid memory of a conversation the two had had one day when Kai asked the old man about how to grow the huge wings he'd need to be able to fly like a bird.

"Don't concern yourself with things that seem impossible," Esmir had said. "Learn to tackle and succeed in doing what is possible, and everything after that can be left in the hands of providence."

What was it that Kai could do? He could protect and nurture the bird, but that was about it. Providence would have to do the rest, whoever or whatever that was.

And so Kai, in his new role as caregiver, began his work. He gathered more leaves to make the bird comfortable and then set out to find some water and food.

Rain had fallen the night before, and some large leaves on a nearby bush had droplets of water cupped in them. Kai cut through one of the stems and carefully carried the leaf to his patient. But the bird was still too weak and frightened, and probably in too much pain, to react to its surroundings, for it took no notice of Kai. "Well, that didn't work too well," Kai mused. "What next?"

He gave up on the idea of feeding, for the time being, and focused on protecting his patient. So he lay down and encircled the little bird with his huge body until it lay snug and safe in its new nest. Kai fell asleep in this position. When he awoke in the morning, to his surprise, the little guy was stirring and chirping in its new home.

"Hey, Bird," he inadvertently named his new companion, though it wasn't much of a name. "Hey, Bird," he repeated. "You seem to be doing all right." With that, Kai uncoiled his body and went in search of some nourishment for Bird, and this time the little patient devoured everything the kind serpent brought it. "This guy has a healthy appetite, if I say so myself," Kai chuckled. Outside of feeding the little one, Kai spent all of his time encircling it and keeping it warm. It was a full-time job.

The thought of Bird recovering brought a smile to Kai's weary face. He surmised that the young fledgling had failed in its first attempt at leaving the nest and taking flight. Somehow, the little one had survived the horrible fall. What was it that Esmir had once said? "If something doesn't kill you, it usually makes you stronger." Being so young and vital, despite its many injuries, Bird was getting stronger every day.

Kai had to confess that he was beginning to enjoy his newfound responsibility, having transformed from being an assailant to being a protector. Who would have ever guessed?

10

A few days later, while Kai was dozing in the relaxing heat of the midday sun, he was suddenly awakened by something tickling his skin. He looked up to find his patient hopping around and pecking on him, as if he was an ordinary piece of wood. The serpent, now turned nursemaid, resisted the instinct to ripple his skin, which would have, more than likely, sent the recovering little one flying off Kai's back and reinjuring itself. Bird probably couldn't know how much pain it was causing by pecking on Kai's still bruised flesh.

"What an insult!" Kai thought, enduring Bird's advances up and down his body. "Only an inconsiderate female would act like that," he reasoned. "Surely, she must be a girl." He lifted his head and looked intently at Bird. There it was, the greatest fantasy of his life—to be a creature that could spread its wings across the sky, take flight, and write its own destiny in the heavens.

In actuality, what was there was an awkward member of this envied species, dragging both its wings behind it, barely able to stand up. What it really needed was a pair of stable and strong legs instead of those fragile and thread-like poor specimens Kai saw on Bird. No wonder she was so clumsy and wobbly.

The gentle serpent straightened out his body and found, to his amazement, that Bird was still on him. When he started to slowly slide through the grass, she braced herself but did not fall off. "She sure is a gutsy thing, the little hitchhiker. Here she is, hanging on to me as I twist and turn through the forest, without so much as a peep out of her."

He turned to a pool nearby for a drink of water, and as he dipped his head into the cool pond, he felt Bird dragging her wings along his neck. "Hey you," he warned when he got his head out of the water. "You're going to drown yourself if you aren't careful."

Bird didn't pay him any mind. She acted as if his head was her head, and as such, she moved about with absolute impunity. The young lady had found a place that suited her to perfection. She sipped from a drop of water that remained on Kai's flat skull and then settled down on the serpent's forehead. With a cozy ruffle of her feathers, she was soon fast asleep.

The long-suffering and patient Kai did not know how to react, but it seemed to him that this impish and frisky little chick was certainly overstepping her bounds and going way too far. Wounded or not, you just don't walk over someone the way Bird was walking over him. Wasn't there a certain sense of decorum to be followed, a sense of decency to be adhered to?

Kai held his head still, searching for a way to rid himself of her clinging tendencies without seeming to have done so. But nothing was coming to him, and all the while, Bird was acting totally unconcerned with Kai's state of mind. She seemed so comfortable on his head, and so perfectly at home with the way things were, that she continued pruning her feathers and softly cooing all the while.

This called for decisive action. Kai decided to return her to the place where he had found her. After all, that was her real home. He quickly made his way across the meadow to the rock where he had first seen her fall. Looking up, he spotted a nest. "It must be hers," he reasoned. Stretching to his full length, he elevated himself above the nest, and with a gentle flick, Bird fell into her earliest home. But Kai couldn't bring himself to leave that place. As uncomfortable as it was, he stretched until he had completely encircled the small bird's nest. Remaining there all night, he made absolutely certain that Bird would not suffer a second fall.

As much as she enjoyed her nest, Bird was much happier on top of Kai's head. With her wings steadily on the mend, she grew to be a constant test to poor Kai's patience. What a vivacious personality this little tyke had. How could someone be so possessive of his time and so demanding of his personal space? Kai was never alone. Bird wouldn't allow it.

The moment she sensed Kai's intention to leave, Bird was instantly on high alert. There was no way he could get her off his body. No way. She dug her sharp, tiny claws into his skull and squatted low, bracing herself for any sudden movement that Kai might decide to make.

He didn't have a chance, and he knew it. As he began to get accustomed to her fickle little mind and her swift and unpredictable mannerisms, he almost began to enjoy her escapades. Almost.

Since Kai slept better under his rock than out in the open, he left bird alone by the tree one night while he went and curled up in his own place. He had just barely fallen asleep when suddenly he was soundly awoken by his little friend, squeaking and fumbling in the dark, desperately looking for her lost bed partner. After that, Kai and Bird slept together under his rock. Actually, it was now their rock.

As time passed and Bird grew steadily to maturity, it became increasingly apparent that she was never going to be able to soar the skies as nature had intended. Although both wings had healed, one of them had a pronounced bend in it that could not be corrected. It caused Bird's wing to drag even as she walked, and the prospect of flying seemed completely out of the question. Her deformity was a bit much to gaze at, but it stirred a wellspring of compassion in the serpent's heart.

Kai wanted for Bird to fly in the worst way. With Bird perched on Kai's head, they would race through the forest with incredible speed until Bird reached flight velocity. As she flittered and flapped to maintain her altitude only a few feet above him, the great serpent followed her movements in pure wonder. She gradually learned to stay aloft on one wing for many seconds at a time. Watching her intently, Kai marveled at her tenacity and the strength of her conviction.

Observing Bird in her struggle to take flight, Kai was reminded more than ever of his overriding and all-consuming desire to experience flying for himself. However, something had changed. It was no longer about gaining power over the sky and dominating the creatures above. Now it was about freedom and being unbounded, and being able to soar to imaginary

realms in real space and time. That was what possessed his soul.

Meanwhile, Kai and Bird had most definitely become an item. They were the talk of the forest. Their strange relationship was genuinely acknowledged and celebrated by everyone who knew them. It bespoke of trust, companionship, hope, and—dare we say—love. Rare indeed.

He, quiet and composed, powerful and majestic, focused and vigilant, and mostly disapproving of her antics. And she, chirping and fluttering about, distracting and annoying, constantly begging for his attention, never more than a few feet away, and always pushing the limits of his tolerance and patience. Truth be known, they both relished each other, at least most of the time.

Kai's only escape from Bird was his midday snooze. Even then, as she planted herself in a nearby tree and tucked her head under her bad wing, one eye was always watching him. The moment he awoke, she was right back on top of his head. There were times when he became downright weary of her constant attention, but ignoring her was not an option. She hopped back and forth on him, kicking, scratching, and assaulting him, and always demanding his affection. The more he tried to ignore her onslaughts, the harder she kicked.

Once, when she started to bite the end of his tail, he'd finally had enough, and the long-suffering serpent lost his temper. He thrust his tail violently. Bird, not expecting the move, was thrown high in the air and landed on her head with a horrible thump. There she was, seemingly as lifeless as the rock she had hit.

For a panic-stricken moment, Kai thought he had killed his little friend and troublemaking partner. Watching Bird lying unconscious, her body racking with spasms, her tiny feet quivering, and her breathing shallow and sporadic, one thought repeated itself endlessly inside him: "How could I have been so reckless?"

Before he could figure out the next step, his heart nearly leaped out of his chest as she began to stir and slowly regain consciousness. She wasn't dead after all. "Thank God for that!" Kai heard himself utter these words from deep inside his being.

Awkwardly rising to her feet and struggling to regain her equilibrium and composure, she cast a woeful look Kai's way. Then, like the conceited lady she was, she began to prune her feathers without giving him so much as even another peek. Turning her back on him, she left in a fit of disappointment. How could he have been so cruel?

Although filled with remorse and grief, Kai could not yet bring himself to let Bird know how sorry he was or how much she really meant to him. In the serpent's long journey from aggression to allowance, he was still too proud to humble himself, even to his Bird.

When she finally returned, after leaving him for what seemed like a lifetime, he felt even worse. He was lying sullen and lonely on a knobby log when he saw her in the distance coming toward him in her awkward way. As she got closer, he noticed a worm dangling from her tiny beak. She hopped up to his face and dropped it in front of him, just missing his nose. Then she sat back on her legs and looked at him without blinking. It was her way of asking his forgiveness for her impetuousness. As for Kai, he made a silent vow to never again let his anger get the best of him, no matter what. Kai bent down to the ground and looked her tenderly in the eye. After a tear-filled moment, he again felt her familiar patter on top of his head. How good it felt.

All was forgiven, and both learned important lessons. Kai would never again object to her playful antics. He understood it was her way of loving him, and it now truly endeared her to him. And as for Bird, she finally came to understand Kai's need for privacy, and she would do her best to grant it, even as the two were becoming nearly inseparable.

For seven glorious years, Kai and Bird explored their forest together. Each day was its own gift, filled with both the ordinary and the remarkable. The two had found a natural ease of being with one another. Their routine was always changing, and yet there was a constancy that felt familiar and secure.

Bird, always her flippant and impertinent self, was forever up to something. Just when Kai thought he had seen it all, there was a new twist or wiggle for him to sort out. How ironic that the great serpent warrior was always being caught off guard one way or another by a tiny bird with a deformed wing. And just as great an irony was the fact that this most irreverent and flighty creature was also the most loyal and totally devoted being in all of creation.

Kai was everything for Bird, and Bird was everything for Kai. Theirs was a love story pure and simple. And the truth was that neither of them had ever been happier or more fulfilled—ever.

11

One evening after the two had spent a particularly rigorous day in the forest, Kai noticed Bird walk off by herself and disappear into a thicket on the far side of the meadow. This was very unlike her, for she never ventured anywhere without him. But the aging Kai was tired and thirsty after the long outing, and he wanted more than anything to refresh himself with a quick swim in the nearby lake.

It wasn't until much later, while still floating leisurely in the silky waters, that he realized that his partner had not followed him. "Maybe she's looking for a little independence," he reckoned, continuing to revel in the quiet coolness of the lake. "Or maybe she's got some bird-brained ideas she's chewing over." Kai chuckled at his choice of words.

It was hard to tell with that little lady. As he reflected on the day's events, it struck him that Bird had not been her usual twittering and chirping self, but that was not unusual. She was very unpredictable and could be very moody when she wanted to be. But, come to think of it, she had not even protested when he had decided to descend deep into an unexplored cave without her, something that was usually unsettling for her and completely out of character.

"Well, I will be especially nice to her when I get back," Kai resolved, as he closed his eyes and drifted in the liquid stillness around him. Sometime later, a piece of floating driftwood brushed up against him and brought him back to reality. When he opened his eyes, he noticed that it was already dark and that a tiny sliver of the new moon was peering above him, reflecting on the lake. He quickly made his way back to the shore, where he was sure he would find his good friend, and he braced himself for a good tongue-lashing because he had been gone so long.

But when he reached their rock home, Bird was not there. It suddenly dawned on him that something was wrong; something was very wrong. It was unthinkable for Bird not to be under the rock at this time of night, since she was ill-equipped to get around in the dark without him. Kai hastened to the thicket where he had last seen her. If this was another one of her pranks, he swore she had gone way too far this time. He would refuse to put up with this sort of behavior anymore.

It had been a long and difficult day, and he was not in the mood for any more antics. He was tired, dead tired, and wanted more than anything to lie down and get some sleep. "If Bird doesn't have the good sense to realize the risks she was taking out there alone in the dark and dangerous wilds, why should I worry about it?" he muttered. But, in all honesty, he was worrying about it.

Kai began searching everywhere for his tiny friend. It was black, and there was hardly a moon to guide him. No matter, he would find her. He must find her. He called out into the desolation, first in anger, and then in a woeful and pleading voice, while carefully scrutinizing every inch of the ground he knew she was familiar with, but all to no avail. He began whipping his tail furiously against the ground, in the hopes that she would hear him. The earth shook, but she was nowhere to be found. For an instant, he thought that he heard her. He held deathly still, not even daring to breathe. But in the end, it was only the stirring of a lonely owl, probably awakened by the clamor.

He had never known such an aching frustration. "Where was she?" he repeated over and over. Whatever pain and discomfort she had caused him was all forgiven. He must find her, his cherished companion of all these years, and then he would never let her out of his sight again. Never.

He poked, prodded, and thrust his tail into a decaying hollow log, desperate to leave no stone, or log, or anything unturned in his search. A cloud of fine powdered dirt and dust covered him. Half blinded, his eyes watering from the grime and terror of the moment, he at last gave up the search and returned to his rock.

His mind raced in a hundred different directions all at once. She was gone, but she couldn't be, so where was she? Was this just a bad dream? It had to be. But why couldn't he wake up and see all of this nonsense over and done with? He had to find her. And why was morning light taking so long to arrive? He finally fell into a fitful and restless sleep, but only briefly. How could there be any rest when she was missing?

He was already up and moving about before the first rays of the new day struggled to penetrate the forest canopy. Instinctively, he returned to the spot where he had last seen his Bird. Suddenly, partially hidden under a white flowered shrub, in a small hole that had obviously been scratched out with great effort by the little missing one, there she was. If not for the streaks on her wings and the disturbed earth around her shallow resting place, he would not have seen her, not even in broad daylight.

But why wasn't she moving? Kai eased up beside her and nudged her head that was partially hidden under her deformed wing, but there was no response. She wasn't breathing anymore. Her body was limp and lifeless. When he touched her, she was cold. It was a horrible cold, and he felt it deep inside himself. He fixated on her motionless body, from her tiny head to the awkward angle of her broken wing. She had dug a small grave in the moist ground, into which she had interned herself, almost as if to save him the task of burying her.

Kai lowered his head beside his darling and now departed Bird, and he lay there, still as a corpse, too stunned to believe what he was seeing, too numb to sob, and too lost in anguish to yet comprehend the irreversible finality of this moment.

After what seemed an eternity, he slowly arose and ever so carefully covered her small body with earth and leaves. He picked a small bouquet of white flowers from the shrub above her and silently placed it over her grave. There was nothing else to do.

Kai hesitated for a moment, reluctant to leave. Never had he felt so alone. Never had his heart felt this heavy. Never had life seemed so fleeting, so empty, and so pointless. Turning away finally, he slowly made his way back to the rock they had called home. Now it felt like the loneliest place on earth.

Bird, his faithful companion, his best friend, and dare he say it, his soul mate, who had for so long endeared and enriched his life, was gone. She was gone forever.

12

The years passed slowly after Bird died, and they were lonely ones for Kai. Every path and meadow in the forest reminded him of her, and every time he heard the twitter of birds, it stirred echoes of longing in his broken heart.

Old age was beginning to take its toll on the forlorn serpent, and increasingly, he felt a lessening of his strength and agility. He was becoming weaker and slower, and things didn't matter much anymore. Even searching for food had become a chore. More often than not, he would just lie under his big rock without eating or drinking.

He still made it his business to patrol his forest the best he could and to keep his companions from harm's way. To his great satisfaction, he no longer saw any of the villagers of Zira. They had long ago decided to avoid him at all cost, and that was fine with him.

The animals, though not openly approachable, did not fear Kai anymore. Truth be known, they had come to value the safety and security of his presence. He had become their friend in an odd sort of way. It was with immeasurable comfort and caring that they watched his huge form slowly amble by them in the meadow clearings. They were careful not to arouse him when they found him resting or sunning himself, not for fear of losing their lives, as had once been the case, but out of respect for not disturbing his slumber and waking him. When they felt he was lonely and in need of some company, they became louder and more boisterous, hoping to raise his spirits and lift his heavy heart with their gentle chatter.

Spring had finally arrived once more, after a long and bleak winter, death and decay giving way to renewal and rebirth. Everywhere, life was reawakening and bursting from its wintry confines. Nature was breathing a fresh breath into itself, and everywhere there would be new colors, new blooms, new beginnings.

The sun was warm. The ground was moist and fertile. The air was a perfume of heavenly scents. And the last remnants of winter's drab grayness were being replaced by a sea of greenish exuberance. Spring had indeed arrived.

Kai had not moved from his rock for several days. He was hungry but too weak to hunt for food. He was content to let the soothing heat of the sun on his back be his sole source of nourishment. He asked nothing more of life than to just be allowed to lie there and be. Just be.

In contrast to his physical feebleness, Kai's mind was still clear and alert. It could move as fast as the wind or be as still and silent as a dewdrop collecting itself at dawn. He could remember everything. His mind could take him back through the pages of his long life and allow him to carefully reflect upon the many happenings and events that he had experienced.

His first tumultuous years as the savage and arrogant tyrant seemed like they didn't even belong to him anymore. Then there were the years of uncertainty about his identity that had started with meeting Esmir. It was a most fortuitous encounter, though challenging and extremely difficult at times. Those years were all like spokes originating from the same hub but without any rim to hold them together and give them purpose. It was a time when only his trust and love for the wise old man had saved him from slipping back into his old habits and wanton ways.

And then there was Bird, dear, sweet Bird. What a great blessing she had brought into his life, so much warmth and happiness. She completed his life in such a beautiful way. Just the thought of her filled his eyes with tears of gratitude as the memories of their years together passed before him. He could remember it all. Such precious memories they were.

One memory in particular stood out and repeated itself over and over. It was that moment when he helped her to get airborne and fly, despite her having only one wing. He marveled at how he had felt himself lift off beside her in his mind's eye and how they had spanned the skies together, experiencing pure freedom for fleeting moments. What precious memories those were.

Now in these last years, alone again, everything seemed to have fallen into place of its own accord, as if doing the right thing had become automatic and was its own reward. Kai knew who he was, and who he wasn't. He had gained so much wisdom from his experiences in the forest. He was aware of his limitations, he understood the stumbling blocks that life presented and had learned to avoid them, and he was consciously living his destiny.

His dreams were no longer wispy clouds in the sky but rather had taken root in the fertile soil of his being. A brilliant sun illuminated his path, free of the shadows of illusion and self-deception. There was still so much that he hoped to know, or dreamed of being, and he knew that he was on a quest that would take him there, and in the process he would discover more of himself.

How had Esmir described it in a conversation that they'd had so long ago? "Life is a journey of discovery, of making known what we do not yet know, and of using all our inner tools of knowingness to guide us along our path until we arrive at the place where everything finally makes sense, and from that place we can see our journey in a greater light of understanding, and that understanding will be the launch pad for another journey of discovery . . ."

Or something like that.

However it went, Kai now knew what it meant. Even his loneliness, when viewed in that greater light, became less of a burden and more of a quiet contemplation into the inner recesses of his soul.

13

The sun was now eclipsed behind a majestic cloud that had suddenly appeared in the western sky. An abrupt chill gripped Kai's weakened body. He made a valiant attempt to move, but his huge mass refused to budge from its coiled position, so he gathered himself even more tightly to his center in an effort to keep warm.

The birds were chirping above him and hovered so close to his head that they almost touched him. He could feel the wind from their wings gently fanning him, and it was a comfort to his spirit. He became aware of the rustling of leaves and the crackling of twigs around him. His forest companions were now surrounding him in a circle of love and support. It touched him deeply. Without being able to see them, for his eyelids were now too heavy to lift, he instinctively knew they were all watching, and this gave him much comfort and reassurance.

Lying there in his last moments, Kai suddenly felt a deep and abiding tenderness well up inside himself for all of these creatures who had shared their lives with him. And beyond that, for all the trees that had shaded and protected him, for the streams and lakes that had cooled and refreshed him, for the meadows that had served as his special resting places, for the rock shelter he had called home, and even for the patch of blue sky above him that he dreamed of enjoining himself with—he felt love for it all. It was all a part of him.

Kai must have dozed off, for suddenly he was awakened by a gentle touch on his forehead. Using all of the strength within him, he was able to raise his eyelids enough to see a white-robed figure bending over him.

Esmir? Yes, it was really Esmir!

The fading serpent tried in vain to react to Esmir's presence as his longtime friend tenderly cupped his hands around his face, put his head gently in his lap, and kissed his forehead. No words were spoken. No words were necessary. For how could they have filled this moment with anything more than was already contained therein?

Time, the great leveler, had been unable to erase this bond. Now even time stood still in obeisance to something outside itself. Their love for each other and their love for life merged together in a rush of pure joy. Years of struggle, and loss, and loneliness dissolved into waves of quiet anticipation.

"It is done, Kai. It is done." Esmir's soft voice reverberated deep within the serpent's being. He closed his eyes again and let the words slowly penetrate into every cell. He felt Esmir's hand continue to stroke and caress his forehead, and suddenly a light from within appeared and began to burnish pure the last vestiges of his earthly life. A still greater wave of energy filled his being and sent his spirit spiraling inward.

Kai let go a heavenly sigh and again opened his eyes, this time effortlessly. Through his fading earthly sight, he saw tears well up in Esmir's eyes. He relaxed his focus. Who was this strange being who had crossed his path and changed him in such a profound way, and had risked his life to do so? Who was he? And now, in Kai's last moments of earthly existence, who was this man who had come to comfort him and be by his side one last time. Who was he?

"Don't you know, Kai, that I am a grand reflection of what you are? I am another yourself." Those were the last words that Kai heard Esmir utter.

A bright, flickering movement suddenly caught Kai's attention. When he steadied his gaze, he noticed a beautiful iridescent form settling down on Esmir's shoulder. It was a bird, of that he was certain, but a bird he had never seen before, or so he thought. He softened his focus. In an instant, he was swept deeply into the serene and penetrating eyes of Bird.

It was Bird!

At first his mind went numb, and he could not accept her sudden appearance. She seemed so much larger than he remembered her being, and her feathers shone with colors he had never seen before. Her wing was no longer deformed but was poised graceful and flawless against her body. When she hopped onto his forehead and he felt her claws gently gripping his skin, he knew without a doubt that his beloved Bird had returned.

A knowing smile came over his face. With Esmir's countenance as a beacon to light the way, the last threads of earthly existence fell away.

A quickening stirred through him. In the twinkling of an eye, Kai and Bird took flight. On graceful, golden wings, they soared upward . . . inward . . . higher . . . and deeper . . . a dream come

true at last . . . only better. Then, in a glorious burst of brilliance, they disappeared from sight.

Kai and Bird, gone together. Kai and Bird, into forever.

And wouldn't you know it? As one altogether improbable love story was ending, an even more wonderful one was just beginning.

ACKNOWLEDGMENTS

Thank you to my husband, Ken, who took a nearly forgotten, dusty, old manuscript and breathed new life into it. Thank you to my snowbird friends Diane and Lenny Hayes for shedding light on Kai's proper spelling. Thank you to Jim Loftus for his wonderful artwork and to Jeanette Little for her fine work in restoring it. Thank you to my dear friend Cynthia Black and her talented team at Beyond Words for giving Kai his own book. A special thanks to editor Lindsay Brown for all her assistance and wise input.

Thank you to my beautiful Ashram business partner and dear friend over all these years, Catharina Hedberg. Thank you to our dedicated and committed staff family of Ashram "angels"—instructors, office staff, massage therapists, chefs, housekeepers, gardeners, and everyone else who brings themselves 100 percent to their labor of love every day. And finally, thank you to every Ashram guest over all these nearly forty years who has made a personal pilgrimage to Calabasas, California, or Mallorca, Spain. Cat and I are grateful beyond measure to have had the opportunity to come to know you and together to create beautiful and heartfelt memories that will last a lifetime.

ABOUT THE AUTHOR

Anne Marie Bennstrom is a remarkable woman. Born in Sweden, she came to America in her twenties and graduated as both a doctor of chiropractic and a doctor of naturopathy. She was the first executive director of the acclaimed Golden Door Resort in Escondido, California. Known as Dr. B, or the "golden girl" of the Golden Door, she was featured in *Sports Illustrated* in 1964 with: "She is a 35-year-old blonde Swede of immense and communicable vitality who eats mostly fresh fruit and can wear tiny jersey shorts. She commands instant hero or heroine, worship, which she exploits by bullying us all into following her through a series of fierce—in fact, maybe impossible—

exercises." Among those she has bullied are the likes of Aldous Huxley, Bob Cummings, Jim Backus, Stanley Kramer, Johnny Weissmuller, Victor Buono, and Sid Gillman.

She is the widow of Robert Prescott, WWII hero and founder/CEO of Flying Tigers Air Cargo. Anne Marie is the inventor of the V-Bar, which would later be made famous by Suzanne Somers as the Thigh-Master, and she pioneered a form of exercise that she called Jumpin' Jimminy. Jane Fonda asked Anne Marie to use and expand on this exercise form, and it later become known as aerobics. Anne Marie has appeared numerous times on television shows as the guest of Steve Allen, Merv Griffin, and Johnny Carson. She is an ordained Essene bishop and has married upwards of a hundred couples. Nearly all of those wedding ceremonies defy adequate description—so much laughter, levity, and spontaneity. She has been a sought-after motivational speaker with women's groups, at commencement ceremonies, and at corporate conventions.

Anne Marie has traveled much of the world as well. She fell in love with Kashmir, a beautiful country in the mountains north of India, known as Heaven on

Earth, and decided to build a houseboat on Nagin Lake. She designed the floating living quarters herself and had it built for her by a family with fifty-seven brothers. In the process, she was adopted into that family and given the name sister Farida (Uniquely Exceptional), was invited to the regional tribal council as a representative for the family (the only woman in attendance), and was given the opportunity to speak at the council (an unheard-of occurrence to this day), where she admonished the "Lion of Kashmir" and his tribal elders for not allowing girls to attend school (much to the chagrin of her family of brothers). Upon returning to Kashmir a year later, she noted that the girls in the region were finally allowed to attend school. A true story, and par for the course.

Along with her dear friend and fellow Swede, Catharina Hedberg, Anne Marie is cofounder of the Ashram, a world-famous health, fitness, and spiritual retreat in Calabasas, California. She presently lives in the San Jacinto Mountains above Idyllwild, California, with her husband, Ken, and Persian kitty princess, Sassypuss.

AUTHOR'S NOTE

The artwork throughout this book was created many years ago by James Loftus, who was inspired to make some pencil sketches after reading the story. Alas, only old and frayed mimeographed copies of his original drawings remained at the time of production for this book. Our editor used the term napkin art to describe them. It was doubtful if they could be restored.

I am very fortunate to live part time in the snowbird community of Caliente Springs in California's Coachella Valley, surrounded by a group of wonderful neighbors, including a fine artist just across the street. His name is Lenny Hayes. I asked him if he would like to read the manuscript and make some sketches that might be used in the book. He was very kind to consent to my request, and he drew the following drawings from his imagination. They're very beautiful in their detail and descriptiveness.

At the same time, the editor at Beyond Words contacted another very good artist, Jeanette Little, to see if the Loftus artwork could be restored from its "napkin" status and considered for placement in the book. Jeanette did a commendable restoration job, and in the end, it was decided to use James's renditions in the book. Be that as it is, I wanted Lenny's artwork to also be included, so here it is. Much love to you, Lenny, and thank you.

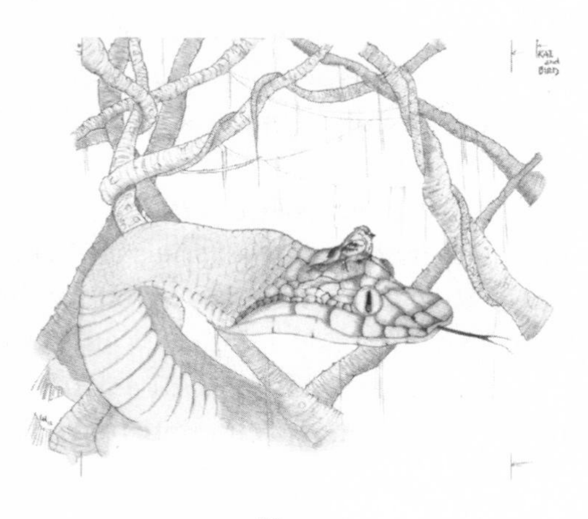

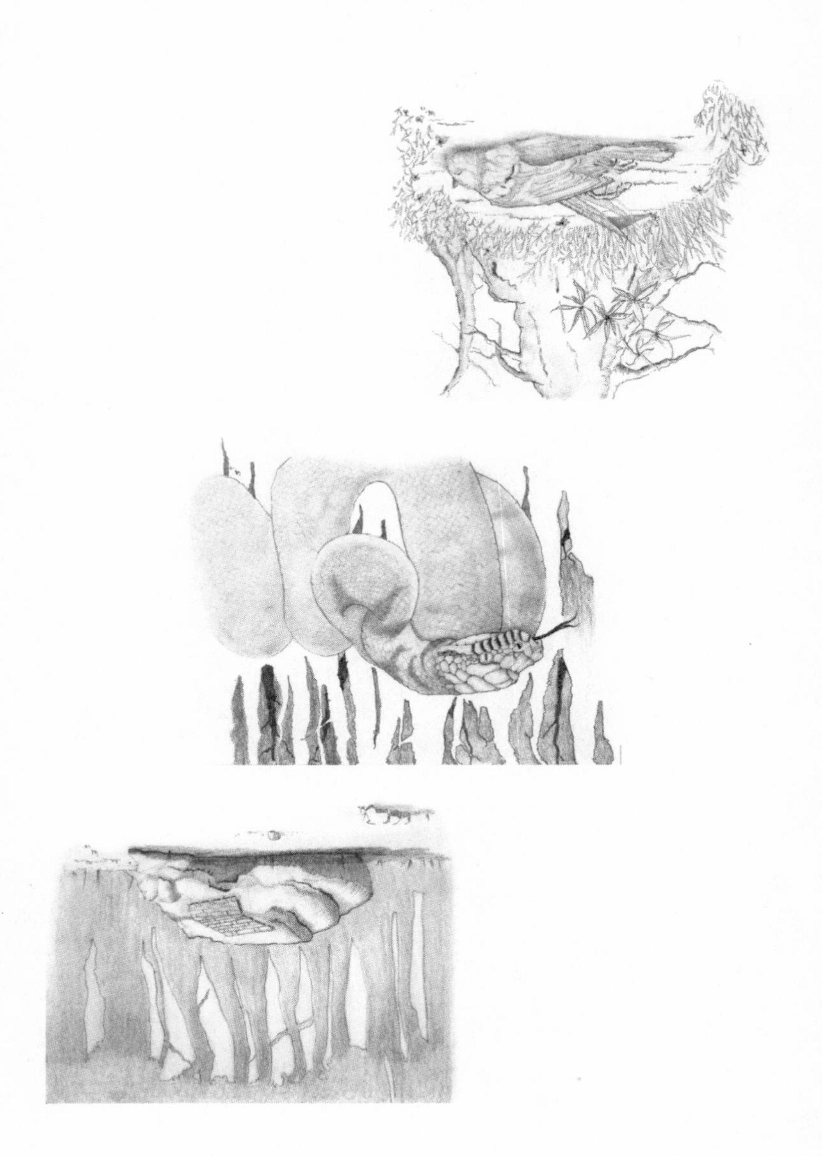

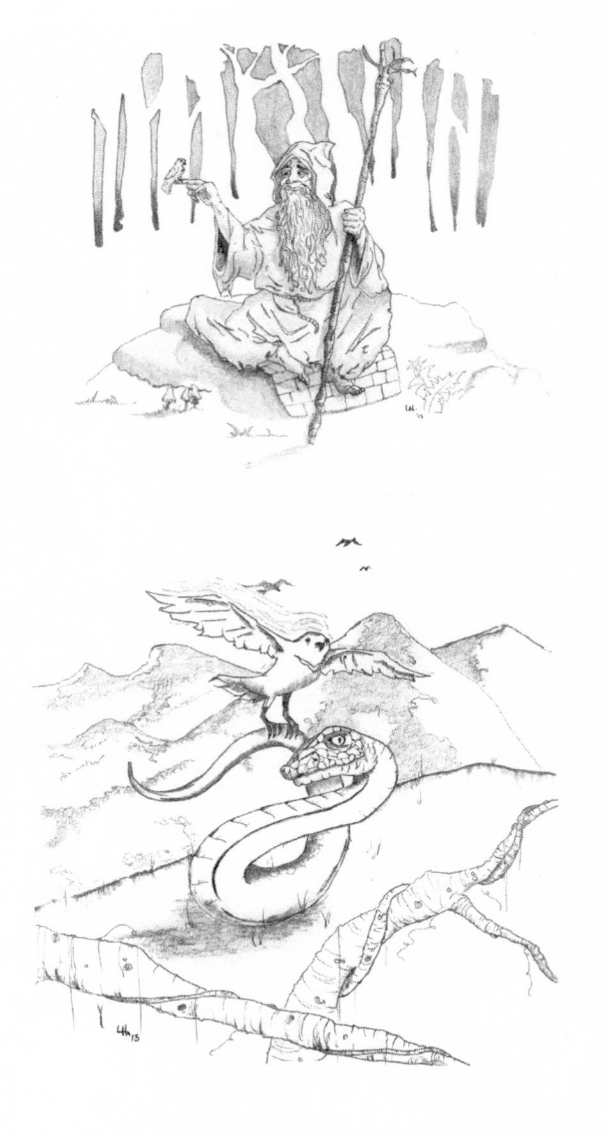